BOG HOLLOW BOYS

Bog Hollow Boys is published by
Stone Arch Books, a Capstone Imprint
1710 Roe Crest Drive
North Mankato, Minnesota 56003
www.mycapstone.com

Library of Congress Cataloging-in-Publication Data
is available at the Library of Congress website.

ISBN: 978-1-4965-4057-7 (library bound)
ISBN: 978-1-4965-4061-4 (eBook PDF)

Summary: Daryl's granny, Miss Denise, has always been known for being a bit of a
cat lady. When one of her favorites, Miss Stella, goes missing, the Bog Hollow Boys
have a mystery to solve.

Designer: Ted Williams
Editor: Nate LeBoutillier

Printed and bound in Canada.
010010S17

THE CATS' MEOW

BY C.B. JONES

STONE ARCH BOOKS
a capstone imprint

TABLE OF CONTENTS

The **BOG HOLLOW BOYS** vow to protect, serve, and nurture the animals in and around Bog Hollow State Park (B.H.S.P.). No animal is too small, large, cute, ugly, slimy, furry, feathered, stinky, or dirty for their attention. Bog Hollow Boys to the rescue!

AUSTIN "ACE" FINCH

Age: 12
Skills: leadership, grit, birds

NELLIE TIBBITS

Age: 12
Skills: smarts, sass, snakes

DARYL "DA SNAKE" TATE

Age: 12
Skills: jokes, wrestling, pets

ETHAN "EL GATOR" FINCH

Age: 10
Skills: tagging along, wrestling, fish

RANGER FINCH

Father of Austin and Ethan
and the warden of B.H.S.P.

DR. TIBBITS

Mother of new girl Nellie
and famous herpetologist

MS. FINCH

Mother of Austin and Ethan,
P.E. teacher, & wrestling coach

MISS DENISE

Granny of Daryl Tate, lover
of cats, & outstanding cook

THE MANLEYS

Bad boy brothers who are
always up to no good

WILLIE AND BUD

B.H.S.P. deputy rangers who keep
a watchful eye on the park

CHAPTER ONE

BIG DAY

As she did every morning, Nellie Tibbits woke up, rolled out of bed, and greeted the four-foot corn snake sleeping across the room.

"Wakey, wakey, sleepyhead," she said, gently tapping the glass terrarium. As she waited for the snake to rouse herself, Nellie stretched and ran a hand through her spiky red hair. Nellie's favorite color was red. It also happened to be the name of her snake.

Before they left Wisconsin that summer, she'd convinced her mother to give her a Mohawk and dye it to match the color of her snake.

"There," her mother told her afterward. "Now you have your own self-defense mechanism."

Nellie's mom, Dr. Evie Tibbits, had taught
herpetology at the University of Wisconsin. She
studied reptiles and amphibians. But her true passion
was snakes. And there weren't many snakes to study
during the frigid winters of Wisconsin. That's why
they'd moved to swampy southeast Georgia.

It'd been a month since Nellie had started school and she was finally getting to bring Red for Show and Tell.

"Big day today, girl," Nellie told the snake. "We're going to teach these Georgia kids the right way to treat a snake."

Red flicked her tongue and seemed to smile at Nellie. Then she slithered inside a plastic pipe. Only the tip of her bright red tail peeked out.

"All right," Nellie said. "You win, Snoozy. But you'd better be up and at 'em when I get out of the shower."

When Nellie got to breakfast, her mom had already put out a bowl of steel-cut oatmeal. Nellie pulled up two chairs at the table, one for her and one for Red packed up snugly in her transport case.

As she ate, she tried to pretend the oats didn't taste like cardboard. Nellie and her mother were both vegetarians, but that didn't mean Nellie loved everything her mother served.

"Eat up," her mom said. "You and Red have a show to put on." As she said it, she ran her fingers through Nellie's Mohawk.

"Mom!" Nellie said, shaking her head. "You're going to mess up my spikes."

"Don't worry," her mother said. "After those kids get one look at Red here, they're going to think you're the coolest girl in school."

"Yeah, right," Nellie said. "These Southern kids already think I'm some kind of weirdo Yankee. Whatever that means."

"You've got to be patient, Nellie," her mother said. "You've got to give these kids a chance to get to know you."

Nellie's mom was always telling her that she should try harder to make friends. But Nellie didn't need friends. She had Red, and she had her mom. Besides, all the Southern girls she'd met were into boys, playing house, and other girly things. They wanted nothing to do with fishing or pet snakes— Nellie's favorite things in the world.

Nellie had tried to talk to the boys in Georgia about outdoorsy stuff. But most of them wanted nothing to do with her. Probably, she thought, they were jealous that she was tougher and braver than they were. You had to be tough to have a pet corn snake like Red. Most boys seemed to be as scared of Red as they were of Nellie.

After Nellie cleaned Red's bowl, Dr. Tibbits laid out the stack of handouts on snake facts. "What do you think?" she said, resting her hand on Red's carrying case. "Think she's RED-dy?"

Nellie groaned and rolled her eyes. "Get those corny jokes out of your system now, Mom."

Before they headed out to the car, Nellie took one last look at Red in her transport box. Red flicked her tongue as if she were speaking to Nellie in her own special snake language.

"Okay, girl," Nellie whispered. "Time to show the kids what we think of their Southern hospitality."

CHAPTER TWO

SHOW
AND TELL

When Miss DeLoach's class started that morning, Dr. Tibbits introduced herself. She told them she was a herpetologist. She asked if anyone in the class knew what that meant.

No one responded. Everyone had their eyes glued on Nellie.

Nellie carefully removed the lid from the top of Red's container. The class watched as she reached in and pulled out the bright red snake.

A few boys let out some *oohs*. A few girls let out some *ewws*.

Someone else called out. "Yeah, Nellie! Bring out da snake, girl!"

"Daryl Dwayne Tate," Miss DeLoach scolded. "Mind your manners, young man."

Daryl waved at Nellie as he squirmed around excitedly in his desk.

Daryl "Da Snake" Tate was the closest Nellie had come to making a new friend. As far as Nellie could tell, he didn't know anything about actual snakes. Every morning he'd show Nellie the snakes he'd drawn on his arms: Larry and Roger.

Though this was somewhat entertaining, the problem with Daryl was that he was best friends with Austin Finch.

Nellie and Austin had already crossed paths. Ranger Finch, Austin's father, was the warden at Bog Hollow State Park. Sometimes, he worked with Nellie's mom as she studied snakes.

Austin was the only student not paying attention. He stared at his notebook as he sketched drawings of birds. He hadn't looked up since Nellie had walked through the door.

Nellie took a deep breath and tried to ignore them both. She held up Red as high as she could. "This is Red," Nellie told them. "She's a corn snake."

Under the classroom lights, the snake's scales winked red and orange. The hourglass scale pattern running down Red's back shimmied. It appeared to move in slow motion as she shifted in Nellie's hands.

Nellie walked around the classroom to give the students a better look. A few kids in the front row shied away and looked like they were about to jump out of their desks.

"You don't have to be scared," Nellie reassured them. "She's nonvenomous. She eats mice, mostly."

As if on cue, Red stuck out her tongue. A girl named Savannah gasped. "Ew . . ." she said. "It flicked its tongue at me."

"That's because she's tasting the air," Nellie said.

Daryl was squirming so much that his desk squeaked. With his hand still raised, he blurted out, "You know I'm a bit of a snake-ologist, myself, Dr. Tibbs."

"You mean herpetologist," Nellie corrected.

"Exactly," Daryl said, still talking to Nellie's mom. "You could call me Daryl Da Snake-ologist."

The class burst out giggling.

Nellie folded her arms.

Daryl ignored everyone, saying, "The problem is that Da Snake ain't got no actual pet snake of his own." Daryl went on to explain that his granny had over twenty cats. "Granny loves her cats," Daryl said. "And she says snakes kill cats."

"This is why Nellie and I are here today," Dr. Tibbits said. "To answer your questions about snake safety."

"And that's why y'all need to talk to Granny," said Daryl. "Da Snake needs a snake of his own."

"I see," said Dr. Tibbits.

Nellie made her way to the back of the class, to the huge heads of the Manley twins.

Hobie and Hunter Manley were pretty much the worst. They'd made up a song about Nellie called "Nasty Nellie from the North."

As she stood there with Red, Nellie could hear Hunter whispering in his brother's ear. "Nasty Nellie, she sleeps with her snakey . . . Nasty Nellie, she's a slithery little Yankee."

Hobie let out a high-pitched giggle.

"What's that, boys?" Dr. Tibbits asked. "Did you have a comment?"

"Yeah, I got a comment," Hunter announced. "Our daddy says the only good snake is a dead snake."

"Yeah," Hobie said. "Our daddy says that you gotta kill a snake before that snake kills you."

The class went silent.

Dr. Tibbits' face matched the steaming red color of Nellie's. Dr. Tibbits took two deep breaths. But it was Austin Finch who spoke up. He'd spun around in his desk to face the Manleys.

"Well," Austin said. "My daddy says that if he ever catches any of y'all killing animals ever again, he's gonna have y'all arrested and thrown in jail."

He didn't make eye contact with Nellie or her mother. He simply spun back around and went back to sketching birds.

Hunter and Hobie started to respond, but Nellie leaned in between their desks. "Do you guys know why Red only eats live mice?" she asked with a big grin. "It's for the fun of it. She likes to toy with them and get their hopes up before she puts the big squeeze on."

Red flicked her tongue at Hunter and waved her tail at Hobie. They didn't say a word. They were both scared stiff.

It might've been the first time in both their lives that the Manleys couldn't come up with anything stupid to say.

CHAPTER THREE

CAT PHOTOGRAPHY STUDIO

Nellie could hear a cat howling before she even got to the Tates' driveway. She found Daryl out in the carport. He had a camera in one hand and a leash in the other. At the leash's other end, a gray cat hissed.

"Oh yeah, girl," Daryl was saying as he took photos, one after the other. "You act tough, Miss Stella, but the camera loves you."

He'd set up a makeshift photography studio. There was a card table decorated to look like a miniature wrestling ring. He'd even hung up posters of wrestlers posing in the background.

"Ahem," Nellie said. "Am I interrupting?"

"You're just in time," Daryl said. He looked up from his camera. "You can assist with Da Snake's photo shoot."

The cat was missing half of her tail and had a notch taken out of her ear. She had a red leather collar and matching leash. Daryl had even managed to get Stella into a black spandex bathing suit.

"Is that supposed to be a wrestling uniform?" Nellie asked, pointing.

"This is Miss Stella!" Daryl said with a toothy grin. "She's a real diva."

Daryl must have read Nellie's eyes. "You probably wanna know why Da Snake's out here playin' dress-up with a cat," he said. "Must seem like I'm some crazy cat person, huh?"

Yes, Nellie thought. *Yes, it seems exactly like that.*

He handed her a stack of fliers. Each one featured a different cat posed in a different outfit. "Eagle Creek is overrun with stray and feral cats," Daryl said. "It's gotten so bad, the shelter doesn't have enough room for all of them."

"Nobody wants to adopt 'em anymore," he explained. "So me and Granny decided to start a foster home for cats. We take care of 'em until we can find 'em good homes."

Nellie took another look at the cat.

It was trying to chew through its leash.

"You really got to find a way to promote 'em if you're gonna have a chance," Daryl said. "You gotta sell each cat's specialness."

"That's cool," Nellie said.

"Yep," said Daryl.

"I mean," said Nellie, "it stinks about all the stray cats. But it's cool that you guys foster them."

Someone honked at them from the driveway. It was Daryl's grandma with a station wagon full of groceries.

She was barking orders before she'd gotten out of the car. "Well, don't just stand there taking your silly cat pictures," she said. "Come give me a hand, young man."

Daryl led Nellie over to introduce her. "Granny, this here is Nellie," Daryl said. "She's that girl I been tellin' you about."

The old lady acted as if she hadn't heard a word out of Daryl's mouth.

"Now how many times I gotta tell you, young man?" she said taking the cat out of his arms. "Miss Stella here can't be trusted outside. She's pregnant and itchin' to run off and have her babies."

Daryl's grandma cradled Stella in her arms and carried her off to the house.

"Don't y'all dawdle," she called out over her shoulder. "These kitties are starvin'."

"Granny, this is Nellie," Daryl said again, this time shouting. "She's the one with the snake."

His grandma had a foot in the door before she looked back. "Nice to meet you, Nellie," she yelled. "Now make yourself useful, darlin'."

Nellie turned back toward the car as Daryl handed her a bag of groceries. Nellie nearly dropped it the second he'd handed it to her. It must have weighed thirty pounds.

"Be careful with that one, now," Daryl told her. "That's the kitties' tuna in there. Hey, you wanna stay for dinner?"

Nellie looked around.

Daryl was still talking as he grabbed a couple bags for himself. "Well, they love almost any kind of fish, and Da Snake likes fish, too. Even though, normally, as you well know, snakes and fishies just do not get along very well."

Nellie didn't bother telling him that snakes and fish get along just fine. She was too busy thinking of excuses why she wouldn't be able to stay for dinner.

CHAPTER FOUR

FEEDING TIME

As soon as she'd brought in the groceries, Nellie was greeted by three cats. They purred, meowed, and rubbed up against her legs.

"Aw," Daryl said. "Making friends already."

With Dr. Tibbits allergic to all things furry, Nellie rarely was allowed to be around cats, let alone twenty of them.

"Y'all gonna help me feed these kitties or what?" Daryl's grandma said. She grabbed four cans of tuna from a grocery bag and slid them across the counter.

"Yes, ma'am," Daryl said.

The old lady handed Nellie a can-opener. "Thank you, ma'am," Nellie said.

"Call me Miss Denise, honey," she told her. "This old lady feels old enough already."

Nellie cranked open the cans of tuna as fast as she could. Five cats swarmed the kitchen table. Four more meowed at her feet.

Daryl stomped back in from the pantry. "Don't be afraid to throw some elbows," he said. "Gotta show 'em who's boss."

Daryl had lined up twenty bowls. "Granny," he said, pouring in the pellets. "Did you know that Nellie's mama's a professional snake-ologist?"

"That so?" Miss Denise said. She had her head half-inside the fridge.

"Nellie's mama lets her keep a snake in her bedroom with her," Daryl said. "Guess what her favorite food is?"

Miss Denise didn't guess.

"Mice!" Daryl shouted as if he was playing trivia. "Fat juicy mice. Just like cats love mice. It's like they were destined to be best friends."

Miss Denise gave her grandson a funny look. Then she turned to Nellie.

"Well, I'm sorry, honey," she told Nellie. "But you're just gonna tide yourself over on some fish fry. I'm afraid we're plumb out of mice."

"Um . . ." Nellie said. She glanced at Daryl.

Daryl rolled his eyes. "No, Granny," he said, shaking his head. "Nellie doesn't eat mice. It's her snake! Her snake eats the mice!"

Miss Denise pulled out a pack of fish fillets. "Well, that's a relief," Miss Denise said. "For a minute there, I thought I might have to waste all this good food on these mangy fur-balls."

They all burst out laughing. It seemed like it was the first time Nellie had laughed since she moved. She didn't have the heart to tell Miss Denise she didn't eat meat.

At dinner, which Nellie couldn't say no to, Daryl kept the snake pressure on his granny. "Nellie here says that cats and snakes can get along just fine."

"That so?" Miss Denise said.

"Well," Nellie said, "I can tell you this. A corn snake like Red isn't poisonous or anything. She can't eat anything much bigger than a small rat." Cats and snakes wouldn't be friends, Nellie knew. But they probably wouldn't hurt each other.

"They can't digest bigger prey," she explained. "A skeleton as big as a cat would kill a snake like Red."

"So let me ask you this," Miss Denise said. She was feeding a scrap of leftover fish to Miss Stella under the table. "You think a boy who can't even remember to lock the kitty gate at night is ready to have his own snake?"

"That was one time," Daryl said. "She came back."

"She came back, all right," Miss Denise said. "She came back pregnant."

She turned back to Nellie. "In your expert opinion, what might happen if a boy forgets to lock the gate on a snake's cage? You think that snake might mistake an itty-bitty kitten for a juicy treat?"

Nellie knew better than to answer that. She looked over at Daryl. He had picked up a cat and was also feeding it leftover bits of fish.

"Oh, shoot," Nellie said tapping at a watch she wasn't wearing. "It's past when I told my mom I'd be home."

"Don't forget the plate for your mama," Miss Denise called after her. "I know I'd appreciate someone bringin' me dinner sometimes."

Nellie wasn't about to tell Daryl's granny that her mother would just as soon eat seaweed as deep-fried catfish.

But it turned out she didn't have to worry about destroying the evidence. She had four or five cats follow her home. It wasn't clear if they were Miss Denise and Daryl's cats or just some other strays.

Either way, they took care of everything except the plastic wrap and paper plate. In fact, the cats' hunger gave Nellie an idea of how she might help out Daryl and Miss Denise.

CHAPTER FIVE

HATCHING A PLAN

Early that Saturday morning, Nellie told her
mother they needed to help Daryl and his grandma.
She explained that the town was overrun with strays,
and nobody was adopting them.

"Daryl says they can't afford to keep feeding
them all," Nellie said. "They won't eat anything that's
not covered in fish, but tuna's expensive. And Daryl
couldn't catch a fish if it bit his big toe."

Dr. Tibbits thought about it for a moment. "If you
are going to catch enough fish to feed twenty cats,"
she said, "you'll need some help from the Finches."

Nellie protested. "We don't need Ranger Finch's
help!" she said. "And we certainly don't need Austin
Finch's help."

"Do you really want to help?" Dr. Tibbits asked.
"Or do you just want an excuse to go fishing?"

Avon Public Library

Nellie sighed and put her head down.

"Well, young lady," her mother told her, "then you're going to have to suck it up. Put away your stubborn pride."

When Nellie arrived at Bog Hollow State Park, she saw Austin at the dock. She almost immediately regretted her decision

"Where's Daryl?" he asked. He looked as sullen as Nellie felt.

"I didn't tell him," Nellie said. "I wanted it to be a surprise."

"Probably better off without him, anyway," Austin said, getting the fishing tackle ready. "Da Snake never stops talkin'. It scares the fish away."

Ranger Finch and Ethan came out of the office. Ethan had his arms full of life preservers. His dad brought a can of night crawlers with him.

"Smell that?" Ranger Finch said. He held it out for Nellie. "The best bait you can come by. Simple, natural, and stinky."

Nellie reached in and dug her fingers into the tangle of worms. She smiled. "I haven't seen this many little wigglers since we left Wisconsin."

"Try not to get attached to 'em," Austin said as he undid the lines for the boat. "They ain't pets."

"Don't mind, Ace," said Ethan. Ethan was Austin's red-headed little brother and the youngest member of the Bog Hollow Boys. He handed Nellie a lifejacket. "Austin's just grumpy. He hates bein' up so early on the weekend."

"Yep," said Ranger Finch, nodding at his oldest boy. "This one needs his beauty rest or he's a sour puss." He fired up the motor.

Ethan giggled. "Yeah, Ace," he said. "Stop actin'
like such a sour puss."

Austin said, "Clamp it, Gator Bait."

Ranger Finch aimed the boat to a spot where
a thick grove of cypress trees loomed over them.
"Catfish love it down by the roots here," he said.
"Bass, too, but they haven't been biting lately."

Nellie reached down over the side of the boat and
flicked her fingers in the chilly water. "You guys ever
been ice fishing?" she asked. "Me and my mom used
to set up our fishing shack smack dab in the middle
of Lake Mendota."

"Nope," said Ranger Finch, chuckling. "We don't
get much ice cover 'round these parts."

"I thought you and your mama were vegetarians,"
Austin said. "Why y'all wanna freeze your butts off
fishin' if you ain't even gonna eat 'em?"

"Same reason the bass masters throw back their
biggest trophies," Nellie snapped. "We fish for sport!"

"Y'all hush up, now," Ranger Finch said. "We'll
scare off all the catfish before we even start casting."

"Don't worry, Daddy," Ethan said. "El Gator is
here, and he's on the hunt for some big cats."

"Thanks, Mister Gator," Ranger Finch said. "We're gonna need all the fish we can get our hooks in. Sounds like old Daryl and Miss Denise got some hungry cats countin' on us."

"Let's just hope we get some hungry cats waitin' on us out here," Austin muttered. He was still loading his worm when Nellie threw out her first cast.

"Nice cast there, Nellie," said Ranger Finch. "A real beaut."

After Nellie reeled it in a bit, she turned to Austin and smirked. "You let me know if you need help hooking that little bitty worm, Ace."

Both Ethan and Ranger Finch shared a laugh. Austin clearly did not share their amusement. He went on muttering to himself as he tried and tried to wrangle that stubborn little worm without success.

CHAPTER SIX

STELLA GOES MISSING

By the time dusk set in, Ranger Finch and
the kids had filled up an entire ice chest with fish.
The ranger had even managed to wrestle in one
nasty old monster with razor sharp teeth. He called
it a mudfish.

He said that normally he'd just throw it back.
"They ain't much for eatin'," he explained. "Taste
like rancid jelly. But I don't imagine a bunch of stray
cats'll turn up their noses at it."

There weren't any lights down by the dock, so
Ranger Finch told them to haul the fish up to the
pavilion. He headed off to the office to grab some
freezer bags and ice.

While his daddy was in the office, Austin pulled
out two fish. One for him and one for Nellie. "You
ever cleaned a catfish before?" he asked her.

Nellie hated to admit it, but she hadn't. She'd never had reason to. She stayed silent.

"Figures," he muttered. "Vegetarians . . ."

He grabbed a fillet knife and cut a line from the dorsal fin to the pelvic line. Then he made a cut lengthwise along the rib cage. The meat was pale pink with little white bones showing through.

"You let me know if it gets too gross for you," he said. "Can't have you puking."

Nellie took a deep breath. "Don't worry," she said through clenched teeth. "If you start to make me sick, you'll be the first to know."

Even after Ranger Finch returned, it took them almost an hour to clean and debone all the fish they'd caught. Nellie got the hang of it all right. But it was past dinnertime when they headed to Daryl's house.

They found Daryl out in the carport with the light on. He had his shirt off and he was posing. He took pictures of himself holding an orange cat in a leopard print wrestling outfit.

Ranger Finch killed the truck lights and shook his head. "Something a little off about that young man, ain't there?" he said.

"Yeah," Nellie said, nodding. *But*, she thought, *in his own weird way he's trying to find good homes for those cats.*

"What y'all think?" Daryl said, hoisting the cat over his shoulder. He pointed at the snake he'd drawn on the inside of his bicep and flexed his arm around the fluffy orange cat. "I call this one Da Snake Charmer."

Before they could think of a response, Miss Denise came storming out. She didn't acknowledge Ranger Finch or the kids carrying the ice chest full of fish.

She was wild-eyed and shaking. She stared at Daryl and the orange cat. "You got Miss Stella out here, Daryl?" she asked, out of breath.

"I thought she was with you," Daryl said.

Ranger Finch asked if everything was okay. "Who's Miss Stella?" he said. "Can somebody tell me what's goin' on?"

"Miss Stella's my pregnant cat," Miss Denise said finally. "And who knows where she could've run off? She needs to have those kittens!"

CHAPTER SEVEN

SEARCH PARTY

Ranger Finch said it was too dark to search for the cat that night. "It's not safe," he told the kids. "Somebody'll end up lost or snake bit or both."

Nellie didn't like what he said about snakes but kept quiet.

Ranger Finch said, "Tell ya what. We'll round up a search party. We'll be back first thing in the mornin'. Plenty of light then."

Ranger Finch did allow Austin and Ethan to sleep over at Daryl's house to keep him company. "Don't worry, D," Austin said. "The Bog Hollow Boys are on the case. Come tomorrow we'll turn over every stone till Miss Stella and her kittens are safe and sound."

Daryl wouldn't look up. "Poor, poor Miss Stella," he kept saying to himself. "Looks like Da Snake really went and ruined things this time."

Nellie surprised herself by asking Ranger Finch if he'd call her mother to ask her permission to stay, too. Nellie knew if she asked, her mother would say no for sure.

Though Ranger Finch sounded nervous on the phone, Nellie's plan worked. Then it was Nellie's turn to feel nervous. She'd just been granted permission to stay overnight at the house of a friend. With boys present.

Miss Denise seemed to sense Nellie's sudden worry. "You come with me, honey," she said. "I'll fix you a nest in my room."

When Nellie woke that morning, it wasn't light out yet. The floor wasn't all that comfortable, but Nellie didn't mind. It only took her a minute to get her bearings before she figured out what had woken her up. Something was rummaging around out in the carport. Miss Denise snored away in her bed.

As she tiptoed out to inspect, she hoped to find that Miss Stella had come back with her kittens. What Nellie found instead was Daryl out digging through the ice chest. On the card table, he'd lined up six chunks of fish.

She pinched her nose at the stink. "What are you doing?" she whispered.

"What's it look like Da Snake's doin'?" he said. "Da Snake gonna set things right and rescue Miss Stella."

He grabbed one of the chunks of fish. He rubbed it around his neck like he was applying fish cologne. "Miss Stella's favorite scent," he said.

Nellie let go of her nose and held out her hand. "Well, then give me some fish juice too," she told him. "I'm coming with."

After they'd fished up and filled their pockets with extras, Daryl asked if they should wake Ace and Ethan.

"We can't," Nellie said. She cupped her ear and nodded toward the back door. A few cats were already mewing quietly from inside. "Those cats get one good whiff of us, and the whole house will be howling."

They set off in the dark. By the time the first rays of light poked through the forest, Daryl and Nellie had been on the trail for an hour. Daryl stopped to sniff the pine needles covering the ground.

"Careful," Nellie warned him, surveying the ground. "There's at least six types of venomous snakes out here."

"Don't worry," Daryl said. "Da Snake knows these woods and every snake in it."

Nellie could only roll her eyes. The only snakes Daryl knew were the two he drew on his arms every morning. And the only scent he was picking up was his own fishy plan that Nellie had gone along with.

"Hang in there, Miss Stella!" Daryl called out from time to time. Nellie just shouted, "Stel-la!"

They hadn't come across any snakes yet. *Most of them are probably burrowed away keeping warm,* Nellie thought. It was a chilly morning. That gave her an idea.

"So where do stray cats go to stay warm?" she asked Daryl.

"Granny says they snuggle up some place that's covered up. Some place where they can hide out and lay low."

"Great," Nellie said with sigh. "So we're looking for the same spots snakes like to hide out and lay low?"

"That's what Da Snake's been trying to tell y'all," he said. He grinned. "Snakes and kitty cats — like two peas in a pod."

"I don't think you've got that quite right, Daryl," said Nellie.

"Shh," Daryl whispered. "You hear that?"

"What?" Nellie said.

"That," Daryl said.

Then she heard it too. It seemed like it was coming from a cluster of bushes up ahead. The sound became unmistakable as they stepped closer.

The bushes were purring.

CHAPTER EIGHT

CLAWING OUT

Both Daryl and Nellie tried to paw their way into the thicket, but the bushes were thick and prickly.

"What the heck is this green vine?" asked Nellie.

"Kudzu," said Daryl. "It's covered in spikes, and it grows everywhere here."

As they searched for an opening, Nellie could hear a low growling coming from deep inside the thicket.

"Hang tight, Miss Stella!" Daryl called out. "Nellie and Da Snake's coming to rescue you."

"*Shhh!*" Nellie said. "She's scared enough as it is in there, plus she's protecting a litter of kittens."

"Ain't nothing to worry about, Miss Stella," Daryl told the bushes. He slapped himself on both arms. "It's your buddy, Da Snake. And he's brought old Uncle Larry and Roger to get you out of this mess."

Nellie got an idea.

"Hey," she said. "Are you going to take your shirt off and let those snakes out or what?"

Daryl looked down at his left arm and then his right. He looked at the tangle of prickers and kudzu in front of him, then back at Nellie. He nodded and peeled off his shirt.

Together they found the closest thing to an opening as there was. It wasn't exactly big enough to crawl through, but it was going to have to do.

Nellie grabbed a stick and poked around for snakes along the ground underneath the thicket. She wrapped Daryl's shirt over her face and Mohawk like a veil. She tucked her arms inside her own shirt.

"You ever seen a snake burrowing in the ground before?" she asked.

"Nope," Daryl admitted.

"Well, you're about to."

Even with her arms and face covered up, Nellie could feel the prickers digging into her skin. It took all the strength she had to burrow through.

When she finally burst through, she was staring eye-to-eye with a notch-eared gray cat with a litter of kittens. Miss Stella looked at Nellie and hissed.

"Nice to see you too," Nellie said.

Daryl dropped to his belly and called out from under the bushes. "Forgot to tell ya somethin'," he said.

"What's that?"

"Try not to touch any of the kittens," he said. "Granny says that if you touch newborn kittens, their mama will reject them."

Nellie looked back at the cat and kittens. "Would you really abandon your own kitten, Miss Stella?"

Miss Stella's response was to raise her hackles, show her teeth, and let out a loud hiss.

"You're not gonna make this easy on me, are you?" Nellie said.

"Well, well, well," someone said from outside the bushes. "If it ain't da snake we been looking all over for." It was Austin.

"But where's the snake girl we've been searching for?" he asked Daryl. "She get scared and run home?"

Both Nellie and Miss Stella let out a low growl.

"You're just in time, Ace," Daryl said. "Nellie got stuck trying to rescue Miss Stella from this here thicket."

"Nobody's stuck," Nellie snapped. "The snake girl is just devising a plan to get these cats out of here without getting them all cut up."

"Hold on tight," Austin said. "The Bog Hollow Boys are here to save the day again."

That was the final straw for Nellie. She might be scratched up from head to toe and tangled up in kudzu with an angry mama cat, but she wasn't about to let Ace rescue her.

Nellie looked back at the cat. "All right, Stella," she said. "We might not get along, but we're gonna have to work together to get ourselves out of this mess."

The cat howled and hissed, but Nellie managed to pick it by its scruff and wrap it like a burrito in Daryl's shirt. She gathered the kittens up in the hem of her own shirt.

She could hear voices off in the distance, but she couldn't tell if they were coming from Daryl and Austin or not. Frankly, she didn't care. She was past the point of waiting for help from anyone.

She could feel the prickers digging into her back and claws digging into her front. "I can't promise this won't be painful," she told the cats. "But I can promise we're gonna get out of here. And we're gonna do it on our own."

By the time she'd backed out of the thicket, she had long red scratches all over her body. Everything stung and itched at the same time.

She could hear the kittens making their little mewing noises as they squirmed around in her shirt. She could hear Miss Stella making her growling noises as she flailed around in Daryl's shirt.

Then she heard the unmistakable voice of Miss Denise. "Well, well, well," she said. "Would you look what the cat dragged in."

CHAPTER NINE

CAT ROUND-UP

Nellie spent the next week licking her wounds. "Look at me, Mom," she said. She showed off the scrapes and cuts that zig-zagged her arms and face. "I think I've already learned a valuable and painful lesson. Don't you?"

"I don't know about that," her mother said. "I think you've got enough stubborn pride to try almost anything twice." Her mother was still upset at her for venturing into the forest before daylight.

"Well," said Nellie, "we need to help these cats, and I know exactly how." Nellie turned her mother's words around on her. "Do you want to help them, Mom?" she asked. "Or do you want to let your stubborn pride get in the way?"

Dr. Tibbits was a tough one. But when she sighed, Nellie knew she had her.

That weekend, one week after the Stella rescue, Nellie rounded up the Bog Hollow Boys. Together, they covered the town with Daryl's cat posters. On the top of each one, they added, *First Annual Eagle Creek Cat Adoption Fair*.

The second thing she did was convince Ranger Finch to hold the fair out at the park. He even made Bud and Willie come in to direct traffic and decorate the pavilion.

Miss Denise rounded up enough crates to house all the cats—including Stella's six new kittens. She reassured Daryl that they were doing the right thing.

"We've had a good run with these here kitty cats," she reminded him. "But they need more food and attention than the two of us can give 'em."

"Don't you worry about Da Snake," Daryl said. He sniffled and cleared his throat. "Da Snake don't shed no tears." Even as he said it, he wiped away some tears.

"It's okay, young man," Miss Denise reassured him. "It's okay. Just let it out."

Daryl could see Nellie and Austin looking at him. "It's okay, Granny," he said with a crack in his voice. "It just clears up room for Da Snake to finally get a snake of his own."

Miss Denise had no intention of letting the boy adopt a snake. They could win the lottery and move into a mansion. There still wouldn't be room enough for a pet snake under her roof. But she didn't have the heart to tell him that right then.

She rubbed the back of Daryl's neck. "It's okay, Daryl," she said, almost whispering. "There's plenty more cats out there that need our help."

Austin and Nellie hung posters on each cat's crate. For Stella, Daryl had used the photo of her in the wrestling outfit. The bio read, "Part lynx, part mountain lion, Miss Stella the Slayer hails from the deepest darkest swamps of south Georgia."

"I thought we were trying to get these cats adopted," Nellie whispered to Austin. "Not start an underground fight club."

Austin eyed Nellie's scratched up arms and face, then turned back to the notch-eared, half-tailed cat. He shook his head.

"You, more than anybody, should understand," Austin whispered back. "There ain't no pretendin' that Miss Stella's some cuddle bunny."

Slowly but surely, the people trickled in. Stella's kitties went first. The kids' teacher, Miss DeLoach, took two of them. Bud and Willie each took one.

Even Ethan and Austin's mother, Ms. Finch, came and adopted one. She said it was time that the boys learned to care for an animal that wasn't trying to eat them for dinner. She stared straight at Ranger Finch, her ex-husband, when she said that. Then to Austin and Ethan, she said, "And y'all boys will be takin' care of it."

CHAPTER TEN

STELLA GOES HOME

By the late afternoon, all the cats had been adopted. All of them, that is, except Miss Stella. The kids were taking down the crates when the last truck pulled up.

Austin immediately recognized the truck. And if he hadn't, he would've recognized the bulldog riding in back.

"Nuh-uh," Austin said, shaking his head. "No way we're letting the Manleys adopt Miss Stella. They probably want a chew toy."

"Now hold on, there, Austin," Ranger Finch said. "Don't go jumping to conclusions again."

Austin begged to differ. He knew that when it came to the Manleys, there weren't conspiracy theories. There were only crimes they hadn't been caught for yet.

"My boys are lookin' for a replacement cat," Mr. Manley said. He mumbled slowly, as if he were talking to the ground. "They say a buzzard got the last one."

Before Austin could blurt something out, Nellie gently grabbed him by the ear. "Just let it go, Ace," Nellie whispered. "We all know it wasn't one of your vultures that got their cat. But this isn't about your birds this time."

"What kind of a cat y'all looking for?" Miss Denise asked.

"We're looking for a little buddy for Bubba here," Hunter said.

Hobie said, "Bubba's been lonely and depressed after Bertha-Mae died. They were best buddies."

It caught them all off guard when they saw a small tear streak down Hunter's freckled cheek. It was the same for Hobie.

"Bubba won't even eat," Hobie said with a crack in his voice.

"Just look at him," Hobie said. "You can see his ribs poking out."

"More like a rack of barbecue ribs," Austin muttered to himself.

Nellie grabbed him again by the ear. She was less gentle this time.

Daryl's grandma pointed at Daryl, who was holding Miss Stella. "Well, we got one left," she said.

"Y'all don't want this one," Daryl said. "Miss Stella's half-lynx, half mountain lion. She's likely to scratch old Bubba's eyes out and eat 'em for dinner."

Hunter said that'd be perfect, adding, "Bubba and Bertha-Mae used to roughhouse all the time."

Miss Denise walked over to Daryl. She reached for the leash.

At first, Daryl refused to let go. He shook his head. "No," he said. "Not her, Granny. Not them."

His grandma gave him that knowing look. It was the Granny-knows-best look. It was the same one she gave him every time he asked for a pet snake.

Miss Denise carried the cat over and introduced her to Bubba. The first thing Miss Stella did was hiss and put her hackles up. The second thing she did was swat him across the nose.

That only seemed to make Bubba like her more. He whined and tried to lick her head. She returned the favor by smacking him again.

Neither backed off or tried to run away.

The slobbering dog leaned way in and tried to nuzzle her. Stella's response was to roll over on her back and take Bubba's entire head in her paws. She clawed at his chest with her back paws. The way Bubba reacted, it looked like she was rubbing his belly.

A minute later, Mr. Manley went ahead and signed the adoption agreement.

"And don't forget," Daryl told them. "Da Snake knows where y'all live. And if he ever catches y'all mistreating Miss Stella, he'll come a callin'."

In one swift motion, he yanked off his shirt and slapped at the snakes drawn on his arms. "And he'll bring Larry and Roger along for the ride," he added.

It wasn't long before the Manleys loaded up Bubba and Miss Stella and drove off. Daryl waved and called out after them. "Keep those boys in line, Miss Stella."

"Oh, I wouldn't worry too much about that, boy," his granny said, putting her arm around him. "If there's one thing I know, it's that old girl can handle her own self."

Nellie grabbed his shirt and dusted it off before handing it back. "Yeah, D. If there's anyone who can put those Manley boys in their place, it's got to be Miss Stella."

"And besides," Austin said, "the Bog Hollow Boys will be lookin' over their shoulders every step of the way."

ABOUT THE AUTHOR

C.B. Jones is a transplanted Southerner who came from the Northern Great Lakes area. When not teaching collegiate writing courses, Jones spends time writing love poems and adventure novels, feeding the dog, and setting bone-crushing picks in pick-up basketball games. Other amusements include Civil War artifact hunting, spelunking, and checkers.

ABOUT THE ILLUSTRATOR

Chris Green is an Australian artist known for creating quirky characters. He has a strong love for bad jokes, great coffee, and all things related to beards. When he isn't illustrating for film or print, you might find him re-inventing the wheel with his 3D printer, playing with power tools in the shed, binge-watching television shows, or spending time with his lovely wife and their wonderful circle of friends.

GLOSSARY

CARPORT — a shelter for a car consisting of a roof supported on posts, built beside a house

CONCLUSION — a decision or realization based on the facts available

DORSAL FIN — a fin located on the back

HERPETOLOGY — the branch of zoology concerned with reptiles and amphibians

KUDZU — a fast-growing eastern Asian climbing plant with reddish-purple flowers; now widespread in the southeastern U.S., it is considered a pest

MAKESHIFT — temporary substitute that must serve a purpose for the time being

PAVILION — an open building that is used for shelter or recreation or for a show or an exhibit, as in a park or at a fair

PROMOTE — to make people aware of something or someone

VENOMOUS — able to produce a poison called venom

YANKEE — a nickname for Union soldiers during the Civil War; still used to refer to people who live in the northern United States, usually by people who live in the southern United States.

CRITTER FILE

CATS

A freshly-spilled garbage can may seem like the work of a raccoon, but it could also be the sign of a feral cat. Feral cats, which live in large groups, often make human habitats their homes, and it's not uncommon for them to dumpster dive for food. It's difficult to drive feral cats away once they establish a territory, and a lack of food will only bring them closer to human homes.

Even though feral cats live near humans, they are timid animals that are scared of humans, and feral cats will hide from most people. You could be surrounded by a whole colony of smelly, scraggly cats and not even know it!

CAT FACTS

→ A stray cat is a cat that is lost or abandoned and was once someone's pet.

→ A feral cat is a cat that was born in the wild to either stray or feral cats. It is generally considered a wild animal.

→ Female cats can reproduce two or three times a year, which means that populations of stray and feral cats can grow very quickly.

→ Feral cats often live in groups called colonies and will hide from humans.

→ Cats can run up to 30 miles an hour (although not for very long!).

→ In the United States, October 16 is National Feral Cat Day.

→ Cats have excellent night vision and can see up to six times better in the dark than a human.

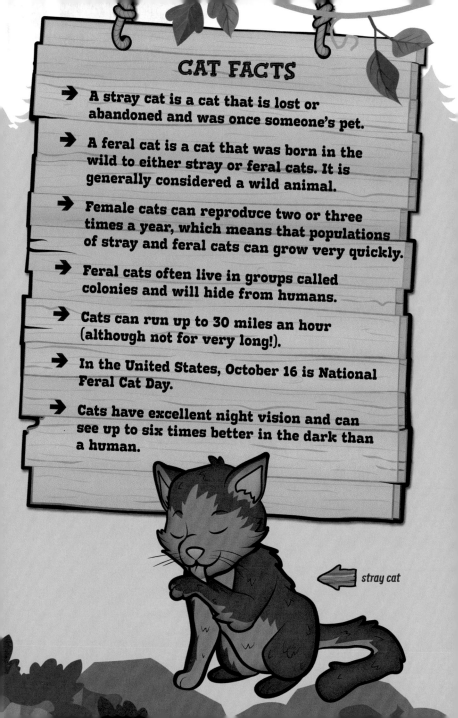

← stray cat